In memory of Mother
        —P. H.

For Alana
    —G. B. K.

A Bill Martin Book
SCHOLASTIC INC. New York Toronto London Auckland Sydney

My Crayons Talk

PATRICIA HUBBARD

illustrations by
G. BRIAN KARAS

Talk. Talk.
My crayons talk.
Yackity. Clackity.
Talk. Talk. Talk.

Purple shouts, "Yum!
Bubble gum."

Brown sings, "Play,
Mud-pie day."

Blue calls, "Sky,
Swing so high."

Yellow chirps, "Quick,
Baby chick."

Talk. Talk.
My crayons talk.
Yackity. Clackity.
Talk. Talk. Talk.

Gold brags, "Fine,
Dress up time."

Silver toots, "Grand,
Marching band."

Red roars, "No,
Do not go."

Green yells, "Fun!
Watch me run."

Talk. Talk.
My crayons talk.
Yackity. Clackity.
Talk. Talk. Talk.

Orange asks, "Sweet,
May I eat?"

Black hoots, "Wise,
Big owl eyes."

White screams, "Most
Scary ghost."

Pink laughs, "Clown!
Pants fall down!"

Talk. Talk.
My crayons talk.
Yack yack yackity.
Chit chat clackity.
Yackity. Clackity.
Talk. Talk. Talk.

Bill Martin Jr, Ph.D., has devoted his life to the education of young children. Bill
Martin Books reflect his philosophy: that children's imaginations are opened up
through the play of language, the imagery of illustration, and the permanent joy of
reading books.

ISBN 0-590-95993-X

Text copyright © 1996 by Patricia Hubbard.
Illustrations copyright © 1996 by G. Brian Karas.
All rights reserved. Published by Scholastic Inc., 555 Broadway, New York, NY 10012,
by arrangement with Henry Holt and Company, Inc.

12 11 10 9   9/9 0 1 2/0

Printed in the U.S.A.   09

First Scholastic printing, March 1997

The artist used crayons, gouache, acrylic, and pencil
on Strathmore bristol board to create the illustrations
for this book.